DISCOVERY
IN THE
WOODS

by
SANDY BARTON

First printing: February 2014

ISBN-13: 978-1490911496
ISBN-10: 1490911499

Cover illustrations copyright © 2014 by Sandy Barton
Book design by Matt Kaiser

THINGS TO DO...

BEFORE YOU READ

Find a comfy place to read, get all snuggly.

Look at the cover. Gather as much information as you can before you start. Get your mind ready for the adventure!

Sometimes it's fun to read with a friend, sometimes it's nice to read alone.

WHILE YOU'RE READING

Make it interesting. Change voices for the different characters. Read parts or the whole thing out loud.

Make a movie in your head as you read. Turn the words into pictures and make them come alive!

Take a few minutes every so often to make predictions. What do you think might happen next?

Remember, predictions are not right or wrong, they just happen or they don't!

WHEN YOU FINISH THE BOOK

Tell a friend or someone in your family about the story- but don't spill the beans, just give them a short summary.

Think about your favorite parts, or your not so favorite parts. What were they and why?

Write a book of your own. Now that's a GREAT adventure!

CONTENTS

DISCOVERY IN THE WOODS

MOVING DAY

Today is moving day, again. The boxes and furniture are in the truck, the neighbors are all here to say good-bye. As I hug each of them, I look over their shoulders to see if Mr. McAllister is coming down the path from the backyard. I have to see him before I leave, just one more time. Another hug, another peek and there he is, walking slowly. I can feel the tears starting to fill my eyes.

My neighbors each walk away and wave their final good-byes. I know we'll see them soon. I also know they don't see who's coming. Mr. McAllister, my little friend no more than ten inches tall, is there. Watching him hobble along the path makes me remember the first time I met him. I'll never forget his angry screams...

ELEVEN YEARS AGO

4

SOPHIE'S SORE NOSE

The ground was soggy from trying to drink up the melting snow, and my boots got sucked into the path, leaving deep footprints beneath the pine needles.

While I struggled to pull my boots up and out of each step, Sophie, my crazy, ridiculous golden retriever, ran ahead of me into the woods. I could hear her sniffing and snorting as she bulldozed her way down the path. As usual, her tail was wagging, looking so much like a golden-red flag waving, smacking bushes and whacking tree trunks. She loved this place!

I had just passed Fort Booga-Booga, the tree house my kids ran to each day after school. They climbed its sturdy ladder to the safety of the perch high in the tree. From there they could see everything - our house, the sand pit, the polka dot tree (that's the tall, tall pine with a bazillion woodpecker holes in it that look like polka-dots), and the acres of woods that we called ours. It was the best "playground" you could ever hope for, and you didn't have to be a kid to enjoy it. I loved being back there, too!

So, I had passed the fort, and the sand pit, and was coming around the bend when I heard A LOT of noise. It was more than Sophie's sniffing and snorting... it was a real commotion! Barking, yelling, more barking, more yelling - the only strange thing was, there were no people around. All I could see was Sophie's big fluffy tail attached to her big fluffy butt, wagging furiously in the air, her head half swallowed up by a hole in the ground. The muffled yells seemed to be coming from that hole, under the roots, under the tree. Sophie was going wild!

By the time I got there, Sophie's head was still in the ground and her paws were frantically digging. That was normal for her, but what was a little weird was the yelling I heard coming from inside the hole. Or at least

I thought I heard yelling! Yes, it WAS yelling - a man's voice with a funny accent!

"Get outta here ya big old brute! I'll show ya not to be stickin' your nose in my house. Take that, and that, and how 'bout a little of that!"

Sophie let out a loud yelp and suddenly she backed away from the hole. She looked so pathetic! Her eyebrows had a dusting of dirt, her whiskers were bent, and her big black nose was covered with mud. She kept scrunching up her face and that's when I noticed the pine needles. If I didn't know better, I would have thought she got tangled up with a porcupine. Six long pine needles were sticking straight out of that big black nose of hers. She looked so funny! I begged her to sit, she did, and I carefully pulled out the prickly barbs one by one.

"Oh, Sophie. What have you done now? Did you chase something into that hole? What am I going to do with you, you silly dog?"

"I'll tell ya what you can do with that big red horse,

you can keep her outta my house and keep her away from my kettle, that's what you can do, doncha know!"

I stood there staring. I couldn't believe what I saw. With one hand holding Sophie back, and the other hand rubbing my eyes, I looked again. He was still there... the tiniest man I have ever seen, no taller than ten inches, and just a little chubby! So, I wasn't imagining it. I really did hear yelling and it was coming from this man, this very little man.

He stood there, shaking his fist in the air. He didn't seem the least bit afraid of Sophie, who was much, MUCH bigger than he was, and he wasn't afraid of me, either! Who could this angry, brave, very tiny man be?

His pants were brown with wide cuffs at the bottom that stopped just below his knees. The pockets seemed to be all stretched out from putting too much stuff in them. His shirt was green plaid, and over it he wore a tattered leather vest. As for his hair, well, it was a mess! I guess that's to be expected when you're only ten inches tall and you've just wrestled with a gigantic dog. I immediately could see how Sophie's nose took a beating. This wee man held a broom in his other hand, a broom made of pine needles, most of which had ended up stuck to Sophie's nose! He shook his fist and waved that broom all the while, yelling and screaming and telling me to 'get that big red horse' out of his yard.

By now my eyes were wide, wide open. This was too much to believe. I was just about to say I was sorry, when I looked down and saw his shoes - boots actually - black with silver buckles. Could it be? Had Sophie discovered a leprechaun in our woods? With St. Patrick's Day two weeks away it certainly was a possibility, but who would ever believe it? The tiny man had calmed down, Sophie was lying at my feet on the ground, and I finally felt brave enough to speak.

"I am so sorry, sir. My dog won't hurt you, I promise. She's a goofy, fast-moving pile of fur, but I can promise you, she's harmless."

"Pinky swear?" he asked.

"Pinky swear," I said.

He stood there looking at me for a long, long time. Then he walked in a circle around my feet, being careful not to get too near the furry beast. He looked up, up, up and pointed at me with his broom.

"D'ya think you could squat down a bit, Big One, so I can look ya in the eye?"

I wasn't afraid of him, how could I be, he was sooo small! So, I slowly got down on my knees, stuck my elbows on the ground and looked him square in the eyes. From down there I could get a better view of his stubbly whiskers, his gold tooth, his rosy pink cheeks, and a hint of a smile. I held out my hand.

After standing there staring at me for what seemed to be a long time, he reluctantly put his hand in mine and said, "McAllister. Mr. C.W. McAllister."

"I'm Sandy," I said, "it's very nice to meet you."

COULD IT BE?

We talked for a long time. The afternoon sun shone like a spotlight through the trees, and every once in a while the light would catch his tooth and send out a sudden burst of shimmering gold. At one point he excused himself and disappeared down the hole, only to return a few minutes later with an acorn cap filled with a delicious smelling cream. He stuck two fingers in, scooped out a dab, and carefully, very carefully, rubbed it on Sophie's sore nose. I heard a lovely, low mmmm-mmm coming from my poor, silly dog and could tell it felt good to her. What a kind thing to do. I had a feeling Mr. McAllister was not so bad after all, maybe a little grouchy, but who could blame him?

He asked me where I lived, what I did, and how

often I came to the woods. How could he have missed the hundreds of walks I took back there, I wondered? But, he had never seen me before, and I certainly had never seen him! (I think I would have remembered!) He liked hearing that I was a teacher and asked lots of questions about school, my class, my family, and if we celebrated St. Patrick's Day. Of course I said yes!

It was getting late and I had to get home. My family would be wondering where I was. I really didn't want to leave; the afternoon had been such fun! My knees were stiff from kneeling on the ground for so long, but I stood up, feeling very, very tall all of a sudden.

"Bye!" I called. "I hope I see you again sometime."

"Bye, yourself, Big One," he yelled back. "Come visit anytime. You can even bring the red horse with ya as long as ya keep her big nose outta my house." He gave me a wink. I turned to walk away, but I couldn't - not quite yet.

"Mr. McAllister... may I ask you something?"

"To be sure," he answered.

"Mr. McAllister, are you... um... I mean... could it be that..."

"Oh for the love of clovers, spit it out Big One, spit it out!"

"Are you a leprechaun?"

"Well, I'm certainly not a talking mushroom, now am I? Yes, m'luv, I'm a leprechaun. A genuine, honest to goodness, 100% Irish leprechaun. Now be off before your family gets to thinkin' that you're lost."

I turned to head down the path towards home. A leprechaun. I had just met a leprechaun. Wow!

an invitation... or two

I was very busy at school and didn't have time to visit Mr. McAllister for about a week. The weather had been cold and rainy and my walks with Sophie were just short trips around the yard. And to be honest, I started thinking that I had imagined the whole thing, I mean really? A leprechaun in my back woods? Even if it were true, who could I tell? Who would believe it? Up until last week I thought leprechauns were make-believe, and I was pretty sure all of my friends did, too. So, I had kept this little "adventure" a secret between Sophie and me.

It was March 16th and the ground had finally dried out a bit, so 'The Big Red Horse' and I headed back to the woods. As we got closer to the polka dot tree, I took a deep breath. There was the most unusual aroma in the air. It wasn't the musty smell of damp moss and wet leaves (although I love that smell), and it wasn't the sweet smell of the pines. No, it was the delicious smell of stew, or gravy, or beef, or vegetables... something bubbly and yummy was cooking, but I didn't know where.

I got my first clue from Sophie. She had learned her lesson; this time she was stopped with her paws right next to the old roots at the bottom of Mr. McAllister's tree. She didn't dare stick her nose in there again! But that didn't stop her from barking and wagging that fluffy tail of hers.

"Oh would ya stop your yappin'! I hear ya and I'm movin' as bloody fast as my legs'll carry me!"

And in a moment there he stood. My little friend. He WAS real and he welcomed us with a quick jig and a shuffle of his feet. I went to bend down to shake his hand and poof - he was gone. Just like that!

"Mr. McAllister?!? Where are you?"

"Over here, Big One, turn around."

Sure enough, there he was on the other side of the

path, stirring a kettle that was hanging over a small fire. Ah-ha, that's where the delicious aroma was coming from. I took a deep, deep breath. Delicious!

"Wait a minute," I said. "but... where... you were just... HOW DID YOU GET OVER THERE SO FAST?"

"Big One, have you forgotten? I'm a leprechaun, and leprechauns have magical powers. We can do things that seem normal to us, but magic to you! Watch."

In a blink he was sitting up on a branch above me, dropping pine cones on my head. They were sticky with sap and stuck to my hair. Great. I tried to take them off, but the sap made them stick like bubble gum, and my hair was a gooey mess. Mr. McAllister thought it was very funny and was holding his chubby little belly as he laughed.

"You come down here," I said, half laughing and half shouting. And poof... there he was, on my shoulder. He touched each of the sticky pine cones and they softly fell to the ground. No stick, no mess, no yanking, no pain!

Hmmmmm, more magic.

"Tomorrow's St. Patrick's Day, doncha know. I'm making a big pot of stew for the family. Would ya like to join us? You can be our guest of honor, Big One. Then you could meet the whole clan - all 157 of us."

"157! 157! There are 157 leprechauns in this woods? 157?"

"At last count I best believe there were 157, yes... with a new baby expected any day now. Why, look down this path. Can't ya see all of their houses?"

"No. I see no houses there, just trees."

"Are ya forgetting, Big One, the trees are our houses? You can tell there's a house if the roots curl up out of the ground like the big old fingers of a giant. We've lived below the trees here for hundreds of years, and we'll live here for hundreds more. So, come tomorrow and celebrate with us. We don't ever have guests the likes of you!"

"Hundreds of years? You just said you've lived here for hundreds of years. If you don't mind me asking a personal question, Mr. McAllister, how old are you?"

"Don't mind a bit. I just celebrated my birthday last month - I'm a proud 127 years old. Now, please, if YOU don't mind, answer my question. Will ya join us for St. Patrick's Day?"

My mind was swirling and twirling and doing flippy somersaults just thinking of eating with a whole clan of leprechauns! "Of course I will. Thank you, I'd be honored to join you."

He must trust me, I thought, and that made me very happy. That's when I decided to ask him my next question...

"Mr. McAllister, would you like to come to school with me tomorrow and celebrate St. Patrick's Day with us? I'll bring you back home in time for dinner. It would be so much fun!"

"You've got yourself a deal, Big One, as long as I have permission to do a little magic, play a few tricks on the kids, sprinkle a little gold dust on their heads for luck!"

LEPRECHAUN MAGIC

The next morning I went into the woods with a VERY big pot filled with dirt, moss, branches and a tunnel dug deep inside. I wanted my new friend to be comfortable and safe for his trip to school. He insisted on not having anyone see him, and I gave him my word. He crawled into the tunnel and we were off.

When I arrived at school, I told no one about my hidden guest. I just put the big pot on the reading table, turned off the lights, and waited for the buses to come. With their usual chatter and laughter, the kids came down the hall and into the room. They immediately noticed the pot.

"Hey, what's in the pot?"

"Why is there dirt in it?"

"What's that green stuff?"

"What's in the hole?"

"Why are the lights off?"

The questions were flying around the room faster than the north wind, and then it happened. The lights went on, then off, then on again. Everyone stopped dead in their tracks, and the room was silent. It happened once more - on, off, on. Then my rolling chair turned in a circle and raced around the room, between the rows of desks, chasing screaming kids to their seats, and back to where it started. Once again, all was quiet. Twenty-five kids sat in their seats and stared at me, wide-eyed, with their mouths hanging open. Since I was sitting on the reading table close to the big pot, I was the only one who heard the very, very quiet chuckle coming from way inside the tunnel. Mr. McAllister was already having his fun. It was going to be a crazy day, I knew it already!

By the time the buses came in the afternoon, we had had THE most fun St. Patrick's Day ever! There was gold dust in every student's hair, there were mysterious messages written on the board, our pet bunny had shamrocks growing in his food dish, and a pale green tint to his white cottontail. He looked a little silly, but I knew it wouldn't be like that for long. And as for the kids? Well, I told them about Mr. McAllister and a few of them were absolutely certain that they had actually seen him in the tunnel! They couldn't wait to tell their parents that we had been visited by a leprechaun. It felt pretty cool to be the first kids ever, to spend the day with a little man with silver buckles on his shoes. A leprechaun in school. Awesome!

AH-CHOOOOO!

The ride home from school was like usual... except for the VERY loud snoring of Mr. McAllister. Goodness - he was so loud the windows were actually rattling. How could such a little man make so much noise?

As I walked up the path into the woods, I could tell my little friend was waking up. The snoring had stopped and the moss in the pot was moving. Suddenly, with a quick "Ah... Ah... Ah... Ah... CHOOOOOO!" the moss broke apart and a piece of the soft green covering blew through the air. There stood Mr. McAllister, a little dirty from being in the tunnel all day, with a handkerchief over his nose.

"Honk, honk! Oh, me allergies are acting up

Big One, excuse me if I have to Ah... Ah... Ah... CHOOOOOO!" Bam! This time he sneezed so hard he blew himself right out of the pot. He bounced twice and landed on his bottom in a pile of leaves. I didn't want to laugh, but I couldn't help it. It was so funny!

"So ya think it's funny, do ya? I have a mind to sprinkle some of me pepper powder on your nose and then we'll see how funny ya think it is!"

"Oh Mr. McAllister, I'm sorry for laughing, I just never saw anyone sneeze so hard before. Please forgive me," I said, trying to hold back more laughter.

"Well, we'd better get back. They'll be expecting us. It's almost time for dinner. Let's go, Big One, follow Ah... Ah... Ah... CHOOOOOO! me. AND DON'T LAUGH!"

I didn't dare laugh, and I followed silently as we neared the meeting circle. The circle was a cleared out area where it was safe to have a campfire. The McAllister clan had made benches, enough benches to hold all 157 of them! Big benches, little benches, (well, they were all little, but you know what I mean) high chair benches and cradles. There were the sweetest cradles that hung from the low branches of the pines. And would you believe it, there was even a seat for me that was a stump of an old tree, two feet high and about two feet across. How they moved it to the circle is a mystery to me, but I suppose some sort of magic was involved! I couldn't budge it myself.

Those leprechauns were pretty clever. The benches were made from branches and they all had pine needle cushions. Some had curved thin branches on the bottom to make rocking chairs. But my favorite things were the cradles for the babies. They were sooooo cute! Made of bark from the trees, they also had curved pieces underneath for smooth rocking. And guess what was inside to make a mattress? Pussy Willows! Rows of gray puffs lined the cradles making the softest, sweetest cradle in the world. I told you they were clever! And in one, was the tiniest little baby leprechaun, the newest member of the village named Meghan Rose McAllister.

Her cheeks were rosey (like her name) and her head was covered with shiny red curls.

The woods smelled delicious and I could tell the stew was ready. There were three fires, each one surrounded by big round rocks. (You have to have rocks around a fire to keep it from spreading, and round rocks don't explode when they get hot!) Kettles of stew bubbled over each fire, and little leprechaun ladies stood by each kettle. Dressed in dark green dresses and pretty white aprons, the ladies stirred and stirred and smiled big Irish smiles. This was their favorite day, and they sang as they welcomed their clan.

I looked up the path. There were lots and lots of little people coming. I could hardly see where the line ended! Tall ones (10 inches), medium ones (7 inches) little kids (5 inches) and babies (3 inches) being carried by their mothers, marching down the path, singing Irish songs and bringing all kinds of food. Oh this was going to be a party!

THE PARTY

I was the guest of honor. Imagine that! After a lovely speech by Mr. McAllister, I was personally introduced to each and every member of the clan. Some of the leprechauns looked at me with skeptical eyes, others warmly hugged my ankles and shook my hand. They were all quite kind to me, considering the fact that I was a.) much larger than they were, and b.) not "one of them". I guess it doesn't really matter what you look like or where you come from, kindness is kindness anywhere you go.

My favorite part of the day, well really my two favorite parts, were tasting that warm, bubbly, yummy Irish stew, and holding the babies in the palm of my hand. They were so small and wiggly; their short red curls were like the flames of a fire and their rosy cheeks were the color of a summer sunset. Adorable, adorable!

The sun had long since disappeared and the stars had poked through the black sky when I said my good byes and headed for home. Mr. McAllister, being the gentleman he was, walked with me down the path, lighting the way with his pussy willow torch and firefly lantern.

"Goodnight, Big One," he whispered when we reached the spot where the path ended and my backyard began. "It was lovely havin' ya with us tonight. I hope ya had a nice time."

"Mr. McAllister, it was my best St. Patrick's Day ever. New food and new friends - I'd say that was a pretty perfect combination. Thank you for inviting me! Good Night my friend," I whispered, waving good bye to a little man, whose life was very big.

THE LETTER

April and May had sprinkled wildflowers throughout the woods. Lady's Slippers, Jack in the Pulpit and Trillium began to burst up through soggy layers of leftover fall leaves, and a few stubborn patches of snow hid in the shade of the tree trunks. The back woods were alive again and the new plants painted the whole place with a hundred shades of green, white, purple and pink.

The leprechauns were also alive with spring cleaning chores. There were roofs to fix, furniture to make and maple syrup to load into the storage cellar in the sand pit. This year had been a good one for tapping the sugar maple trees. The buckets that had hung on the trees during the warm days and chilly nights of March, collected the drip, drip, dripping sap. Once the buckets had been gathered, the sap was boiled down into golden syrup. Thankfully, there were hundreds of jars of that delicious sticky stuff waiting to be put away.

I visited Mr. McAllister at least a couple of times each week that spring. We always had a good talk as we walked through the woods on those fresh days. But, there was a day in early June that was not so pleasant. Before going back to the woods for a visit, I sat on the front steps sorting through the stack of mail that had just been delivered. I noticed a large yellow envelope. It looked very important, so I ripped it open, curious to see what it was. The other mail slowly slid off my lap as I read the words on the paper.

Dear Resident:

This letter is to inform you of re-zoning plans for the wooded area behind your house.

Please be advised that a developer has purchased the property and will begin clearing the woods on October 1st to make way for new homes. It is extremely important that you keep away from

this area while the trees are being cut down.
Big trucks, powerful saws and falling trees
will make it very dangerous for anyone back there.

Thank you for your cooperation.

Sincerely,
Ace Builders

I sat there staring at the letter for what seemed like a long time. Cutting down the woods... big trucks... falling trees... dangerous. Oh no! The beautiful woods - gone? And the leprechauns - they were in real danger! I had to talk to Mr. McAllister immediately!

BAD NEWS

"Mr. McAllister, Mr. McAllister! Are you back here? Come quick! I have to talk to you!" I was frantic. Running through the woods, I tripped over a branch and fell flat on my face. Luckily I missed Mr. McAllister by about six inches. He was just coming around the corner when I landed on the ground.

"What's the hurry, Big One? Sounds like the sky is falling!"

"It is!" I screamed. "The sky AND the trees!"

"Slow down... what are you talkin' about?"

"Oh, Mr.McAllister," I began, "something awful has happened. Here, sit down and let me explain."

I knew it would break his heart, but I had to tell him. I read him the letter. The look on his face made me so sad. His home was going to be destroyed. These woods, the flowers, the trees, the sand pit, the meeting circle, all of it - cut down to build new houses. He hung his head and very quietly began to cry. Tears splashed on his dirty boots and trickled to the ground.

"Why? Why, Big One? What will we do?" Mr. McAllister looked up at me.

For the first time since I had known him, he looked scared, confused and maybe even out of magic.

"Don't worry. We'll think of something," I said, not even believing myself. "But for now, I have to get back home, it's almost time for dinner. I think we have to have a family meeting ... maybe you'd better do the same. Can we meet again tomorrow? I promise we'll figure this out. I promise."

"Of course, Big One. We'll figure it out. I'll be here tomorrow at 4 o'clock."

I could barely stand to watch him as he walked away. He was so sad. It's a terrible feeling to see a friend so upset and not be able to help. There had to be something we could do. A family meeting after dinner was a start. Maybe if we all put our heads together, we could come up with an answer. But that was a BIG maybe.

a Family Meeting

When the dinner dishes had been washed and the kitchen was clean, I called everyone into the family room. Not quite sure how to begin, I told them about my day, then gradually got to the letter and read it, without looking up. I couldn't stand the thought of seeing their faces.

"...and so that's it. They're tearing the woods down to build fancy new houses," I said, folding the letter and putting it back into the envelope.

There was silence for a minute, maybe two. The kids started asking questions about the sand pit, Fort Booga-Booga, the secret hide-outs and of course, the leprechauns. I had no answers except to say that it was all happening and it would start in October.

That same night, Mr. McAllister and the people in his village were hearing the news. They had a much bigger problem though. This was their home, not just their back woods. They were stunned as they listened to Mr. McAllister explain, and agreed to go back to their homes and think about it. Hopefully someone would come up with a solution. After all, they could move to the woods across the railroad tracks. There weren't as many trees, and it would take a long time for it to feel like home, but at least it wouldn't be too far away. Of course, cars and roads and people-chatter would replace the peaceful beauty of the woods they loved, but it was a place to live.

Back at my house, the conversation had turned very serious; we all wondered what it would be like to look out of our back windows or to sit on the deck and see nothing but gigantic houses instead of our beautiful woods. Is this what we really wanted? Would we be able to build a new tree fort somewhere else? Would it even seem like home? It was a difficult decision to make, but by the end of the evening we had agreed on our solution. The next step would be telling Mr. McAllister about it. I was dreading our 4 o'clock meeting. Tears ran down my face. This was going to change everything, and my heart felt so sad.

PINKY SWEAR

The school day zoomed by and before I knew it I was heading home to meet with Mr. McAllister. The sun was hot as I walked through the backyard to the path, and my mind was racing with words, practicing how I would say what I had to say.

Damp, shady, musty air told me that I was on the path. I made my way through the hallway of tall pines, past the sand pit and finally stood in front of Mr. McAllister's home. The gnarled roots that grabbed at the mossy ground near my feet almost seemed to say - *Nope, we're staying right here. Nothing's going to make us move, not bulldozers, not chainsaws, not men in big trucks - nothing.*

"Hello, Big One. How was your day?"

"Not too good," I said sadly. I think he knew that before he asked.

We sat together on the logs at the meeting circle, both looking at the ground for what seemed like a long time. Neither one of us said a word. Then I broke the silence...

"We're going to move." The words just fell out of my mouth before I had a chance to think. "We can't stand to think of looking at all of this... gone. We're going to try to find a new home with woods, and flowers, and, well, you know, all of the beautiful things that made this place so special. It won't be the same, but at least it will be better than looking at giant, new houses. That's what we've decided, Mr. McAllister, how 'bout you? What will you do?"

He cleared his throat. "Well, we all agreed that the best thing is for us to move across the railroad tracks, away from the new houses and closer to the creek. I went there last night to see if there's enough room for all of us, and I think it will be ok, a little crowded, but ok. We'll be fine, Big One, don't worry about us. The only thing I'm worried about is if I'll ever see you again. Will you come to visit? Will we still tell each other stories? Will you remember me once you've gone?"

"Of course I will you silly little leprechaun! How could I forget you? How could I not come to visit, and hear stories, and tell you mine? I'll come to visit you every week, I promise."

Mr. McAllister held out his pinky... which, by the way, was a really, really tiny pinky! "Pinky swear, Big One?" I held out my pinky and hooked it around his.

"Pinky swear, Mr. McAllister."

"Then be off with ya'. You've got to find yourself a new house, so ya better be goin. Go, scat... and doncha be lookin' so sad. The luck o' the Irish you'll have, ya know. You'll find a place to call home. It'll be perfect. And Big One ... doncha know how much I'll miss ya?"

"Yea, I know. I know exactly." I couldn't look back, and I couldn't see ahead of me. The tears made everything a blurry mess.

A TEACUP AND A DREAM

Summer in the woods was magical. Our family spent lots and lots of time with the leprechauns. There were parties and celebrations, four new babies, contests and races and just plain quiet evenings around the fire with our little friends. We treasured each and every moment of the summer because we knew it would be our last in that magical woodland. We tried not to be sad; we wanted to remember happy times and did our best to be the happiest, craziest, goofiest friends we could be. And it worked. The summer was magical.

Finding a new house wasn't nearly as easy as I thought it would be. We looked and looked but there was always something very wrong. The house was too small, the garage was falling down, the woods only had three trees, there was no place for a garden, the house was older than George Washington and was crumbling, or there was no place to build a new tree fort.

Then one day in July, I was driving down a street that ran along the banks of a wide creek. I saw a garage sale sign and followed the arrows to a big white farmhouse, with tables and tables and tables of stuff for sale. I parked the car in front of the house and walked up the driveway that went from the road, around the back, and then out to the road again. I noticed the backyard. There was a huge pool, a gigantic lawn and behind the neatly mowed grass... woods. Hundreds of tall trees with leaves rustling in the summer breeze. The whole place was beautiful and I immediately envied the people who lived there. I wondered if they knew how lucky they were?

Meanwhile, back at the tables I found a pretty little teacup that had tiny yellow flowers painted on the white china. It would look lovely with my collection of cups and saucers, so I grabbed some money from my purse and went to pay.

"You sure have lots of things for sale! I think I'll take this teacup, please. How much is it?" I asked.

"Oh that was my grandmother's favorite cup. It's $10.00."

I thought it was a little expensive, but I could understand that it must have been special to the family. So, why were they selling it, I wondered?

"Here ya go," I said, handing over the money. "I love your yard - it's beautiful. And your house is charming. Old farmhouses are my absolute favorite things!"

"If you like it so much, you can buy it," the lady laughed, thinking she was making a funny joke. "It's for sale, but we haven't put up the sign yet. Want to see inside?"

I had a weird tingly feeling and at that moment I knew I had found our new house. I followed her across the front porch, through the kitchen with brick walls, down the halls with wide-planked floors, up the creaky stairs, and into every room of that old, lovely home.

I wanted it. I wanted to bring my family to see it. I wanted to live by those woods and breathe in the sweet scent of pine trees and musty woods. I wanted it.

The car must have driven itself home that day because I don't remember how I got there, but I do remember running into the house screaming, "Leprechaun magic! Leprechaun magic! That's what led me to the most beautiful house and woods, and yard, and creek... I FOUND OUR NEW HOUSE!!!!!"

There was so much jumping and shouting and yelling and screaming that the whole house seemed to shake. I knew that everything was going to be ok, just like Mr. McAllister had said it would be. Maybe even perfect. Almost at once all four of us stopped jumping and stared at each other.

"It has a woods? A BIG woods?"

"Yes."

"It has a creek? A BIG creek?"

"Yes."

"It has a a backyard, a pool AND a good old house?"

"Yes. Yes. YES!"

And then we all shouted at once, "Then they can come with us!"

I knew I couldn't wait until the next morning to tell Mr. McAllister our idea, so I went back that night to find him. He was where I thought he'd be, sitting by the fire with his family and friends. The smoke swirled in gray wavy lines like kite tails, up, up and disappeared into the star-filled sky. The babies rocked softly in pussy willow cradles, the fireflies danced on the path, leaving sparks of light to show where they'd been, and the little kids played hide 'n seek behind the tall pines. Oh, I knew I was going to miss this place, and so were they, but I had some exciting news to share!

a MILLION TIMES, YES

"Mr. McAllister?" I whispered.

"Oh, good gumballs Big One!" he shouted. "You scared the boots right off of my feet. What in the world are you doing back here so late at night?"

"I have to ask you a very important question," I said, "and I don't want you to answer it tonight. Promise me you'll think about it."

"I promise."

"I found a house today. It's a perfect old house with creaky stairs and wide-planked floors, lots of bedrooms, a nice backyard, a pool, a creek AND a huge woods."

"I'm happy for you, Big One," Mr. McAllister said softly.

"You don't sound happy," I said.

"I am, but I can't pretend that I won't miss you. You're the biggest friend I have, well, I mean, you are big, but you're also my good friend. That's why I'm happy for you, and sad for me."

"Well then, I guess it's time to ask my question. Are you ready?"

"Ready? Ready for what?"

"We were wondering if you, I mean all of you, want to move with us."

"To the new house?"

"Yes, to the new house."

"With you?"

"Yes!"

"To the new woods?"

"Yes!"

"With you?"

"YES. A million times, YES!"

"Oh my good gumballs. That's some question! Leave here? This is the only place we've ever known. Moving across the tracks to the creek is one thing, but moving to another town, well, that's a big decision. I don't know. Oh my. Goodness gracious. Um... You're right. I will have to think about it and ask the others. Big One, this is a big one!"

"Think about it and we'll talk later. For now, go back to the fire, and I'll see you tomorrow at 4 o'clock. You can tell me your answer then. Sound fair?"

"Fair enough."

Mr. McAllister walked with me to the end of the path, lighting the way with his firefly lantern.

"And Big One?"

"Yes?"

"Thank you for being my friend. Only a good friend would worry about us and care enough to invite us to come along to a new place."

"The pleasure's all mine," I said and walked home in the dark night.

GUMBALLS IN YOUR HEAD

I was so anxious to hear what the answer would be and thought about it all day. First I'd think yes, of course he'd want to come with us. Then I'd think no, no way would he want to leave his home. Yes, no, yes, no. I knew I'd have to just wait and see.

As I walked to the woods I noticed something was different. It was really, really quiet. Usually there was some kind of noise or some scurrying about under the pine needles, but today there was nothing. I walked and listened, and walked further, and listened and stopped. Then poof! Like magic, there he was in front of me. "Fancy meeting you here!" he shouted.

I could tell he was in a goofy mood by the way he was disappearing and then popping up somewhere else.

Leprechauns. Crazy leprechauns.

"Would you please stop that, at least long enough to talk?" I asked. "You're making me dizzy!"

"Certainly, be there before ya can say, "Polish me buckles and crack all me knuckles!"

In no time he came out from under a prickly bush. He had burrs all over his clothes and in his hair, and he did a funny little jig as he tried to get them out of his britches.

"Ouch, yeech, oooooh, good gumballs those hurt! Next time I'll have to do me magic in a better spot!"

"Mr. McAllister, I can't wait any longer. What is your answer?"

"Hmmmm. My answer? Well ya see, I would miss this place if I left. We would all miss this place."

My heart sank.

"But ya know, I would miss you more if I didn't go, than I'd miss this place if I did go."

"So? Does that mean that you're coming with us?" I screamed.

"No. It doesn't mean that I'm coming with you."

"I don't understand," I said.

"I'm not coming.... WE'RE coming! WE'RE ALL coming!"

"All of you?"

"ALL OF US!" they shouted. The entire village, all 160 of them, had been listening from the branches of the trees, and now they were jumping up and down, and the branches of the pines bounced under the weight of their happy little feet. Showers of pine needles rained down as we danced and jumped for joy. Leprechauns were popping up everywhere, why some even landed on my shoulder and danced a jig. (Let me tell you... that tickled!)

When things had settled down, we went back to the circle to talk about the move. They were all very excited and a little nervous, too. After all, this would be a BIG deal for them. So many leprechauns, so much stuff. I knew one thing for sure - we'd have to plan this very carefully.

"Mr. McAllister, I'm assuming you can all just do a little magic and poof yourselves over to the new house, right?"

"What do you think I am, a flying pig? No we can't do that. We're moving to another town... with all of our belongings... and ya think we can just 'poof' ourselves from here to there? Do ya have gumballs in your head, Big One?"

"Oh my," I said. I hadn't thought about how we'd get them to our new place. Hmmm."Ok, well, let's see. I have a van. Do you think you'd all fit in it? You and all of your stuff?"

"I think we would, but they've never seen the likes of a car. I rode in it with you to school, but they'd probably go a little on the crazy side if they had to ride in one, ya know."

"Well, I don't see how else we can do it, so it's decided. In the van you'll go!"

He was right, they did go a little crazy. Some were excited, some were scared, some thought the car would eat them, some thought it might spin and make them dizzy. One thing was for sure - they were excited about moving with us to a new home and they started packing immediately.

For the next two months my family packed, too. We packed up our plates and our toys, our lives and our memories. We said goodbye to friends and to the beautiful old house that had wrapped itself around us for ten years. It was hard leaving, but nothing stays the same. We had a new adventure ahead of us... and we were taking 161 friends along!

Our moving day was busy. The big moving van was filled from front to back and side to side, and soon there wasn't room for one more thing. Yikes! Who knew we had so much stuff? The most important things were in the car and the van: my husband, my two kids, the dog, four guinea pigs, an aquarium full of floppy plants and a bunch of fish in plastic bags filled with water. We were ready.

Before we left, I ran to the woods to say goodbye.

Luckily it was just goodbye for a day. I would be back in the morning for the whole village of leprechauns. Yes, a whole village in my mini van... yeech! Now that was going to be a sight.

FINALLY HOME

I was exhausted. That night, after a long day of moving, we slept in sleeping bags on the mattresses - flat on the floor. I couldn't find the boxes that had sheets in them, and I couldn't find the blankets either. But that was ok. I thought it was more important to get the guinea pigs in their cages, and the fish out of their plastic bags. They seemed to agree. The guinea pigs squealed their thanks as they chewed on new toilet paper rolls, and the fish swam a bazillion laps in the sparkling clean aquarium. Now all I had to do was move 161 leprechauns from the old woods to the news woods.

In the morning I stood in the family room and looked out of the window. It was early October and the leaves were beginning to do a little magic of their own.

Reds and golds dripped from their branches while the pines, ever green and tall, stood proudly in two straight lines. There was a blanket of golden needles that carpeted the ground between those two straight lines, barely covering the gnarled fingers of roots that grabbed the ground at the bottom of each tree. It was like a yellow brick road for as far as you could see, a perfect home for leprechauns. I couldn't wait for them to see it!

I drove to our old house, and slowly, slowly backed into the driveway, around the side of the garage, through the backyard and up to the woods. The leprechauns were not there, but piles of chairs and cradles, pots and pans, lanterns and firewood, suitcases and boxes lined the path. I opened the back of the van and started loading their things. Smelling smoke I turned around to see a long, long line of little people - all shapes and sizes, coming down the path carrying pussy willow torches. It was their way of saying goodbye to their home. I felt a little sad for them, but didn't want to let them see me looking weepy, so I just kept loading the van. When it was time to get them in... well, let's say it stopped being sad and started being the funniest thing I had ever seen.

I leaned a long piece of wood from the ground to the bumper and they were able to walk up the ramp easily, so easily that they started running, then hopping, then playing leap frog, then falling off and having to start again. Men were dangling from the side, babies were crawling up, ladies were trying to carry kids, oh it was a crazy sight. Once everyone was in (and yes, they did all fit!) we had a slight problem. Although they blew the torches out before they got in, the ends were still smoking and soon the car was filled with smoke. Opening the windows helped, but then they started complaining because they were cold. I couldn't start driving because Mr. McAllister was swinging from my rearview mirror, his friend was sitting on the steering wheel, there were kids sliding down the radio knobs so the stations were all messed up, and the volume was getting loud and soft, loud then soft. There were little eyes staring at me from behind the heating vents, there were babies sitting in the cup holders, there were even leprechauns sitting on the headrests of the seats. Then the windows started going up and down, but I discovered that was because someone was sitting on the automatic window buttons and had nothing to do with leprechaun magic.

Once I got everyone to sit down in safe places, we were ready to go. All 162 of us were looking out the windows as we drove away; it was quiet... for about a minute. Then a thunderous roar went up as we turned the corner and headed to our new home. There was singing, and clapping - no dancing because I said they had to stay seated - and I saw nothing but happy faces when I looked into my rearview mirror. This was going to be a good day!

Mr. McAllister insisted on honking the horn as we pulled up to the "new" old house. Everyone came out to greet us... even the dog! Unloading was much easier than loading had been. The leprechauns formed a long line from the car to the woods, and passing things along from hand to hand worked nicely. Families split up and headed down the 'yellow brick road' to choose houses. There were plenty of trees for everyone and just hearing how happy they were made my heart smile. When the day was over, they were settled, they were tired, and best of all, they were finally home.

LEPRECHAUN OLYMPICS

By the end of fall the leprechaun village was a beautiful creation of vines, and bark, of clearings and tiny docks along the creek. The men had built rafts and boats. The kids had built forts and tree houses. There were meeting circles and schools, churches and supply huts. It was about as perfect a place as you could imagine. And best of all, we saw each other often!

The leprechauns had a brilliant way of letting me know if something important was happening. A mourning dove named Rosie agreed to carry messages from the woods to my back door. Rosie never spoke to me, but somehow she managed to communicate with the leprechauns. She'd peck on the window when she had a note for me, and then I'd know to look for it. Sometimes we'd leave cornbread out for her; it was her favorite treat. What seemed to be a huge, gigantic, horrible problem back in June had turned out to be a wonderful blessing instead. Life was good at the new house.

When winter finally came, it stayed and stayed and stayed, and snowed and snowed and snowed. Poor Mr. McAllister. One day I went back to see him, and lucky for him that I came when I did. I heard a bunch of mumbling and couldn't quite figure out what it was. As I got closer to his house I noticed feet kicking in all directions from a snow bank. It was Mr. McAllister. He had been trying to fix his leaking roof, had fallen off of the ladder and landed head first into a huge pile of snow. I dug him out and wrapped him in my scarf to warm him up for a bit. He did look funny upside down in that pile of snow, but I didn't laugh... at least not until I got back to my house!

The winter highlight came in February with the first annual Leprechaun Olympics! There were luge races, snowball throwing contests, ice skating, log skidding, down-hill skiing competitions, dog-sled races and catapulting. I'm not sure which event was my favorite, but I can tell you this, I've never heard louder cheering than I did for the catapulting. My goodness!

Our backyard was divided up into different areas for the events. On any of the Olympics days, we could look out of the windows and see crowds of leprechauns cheering for their favorite races. There was never a fear of the neighbors hearing or seeing anything because our houses were pretty far apart. The little folks were free to have their games in peace.

Everyone in my family had very important responsibilities at the Olympics - even the dog. For example, the dog sled event required Sophie's help. Mr. McAllister had handcrafted a sled out of bark and branches. It was beautiful. Attached to the front were two long pieces of rope. We tied the ropes to Sophie, and held her until a leprechaun climbed into the sled. Then we threw a tennis ball all the way across the yard and let her go. Sophie went running like a race horse, with the leprechaun holding onto the sides of the sled for dear life. Whoever stayed in the sled the longest without being thrown out by the flipping and flopping that Sophie caused, was the winner. Sometimes the sled turned over three or four times in one run! And sometimes it looked more like a rodeo than a winter Olympic event!

The catapult was amazing and was probably my favorite event, but it was definitely the most dangerous. The contestants were very brave and had to wear helmets because it involved flying! I was in charge of this event, but it made me a little nervous when I heard what would be happening.

We stuck a tennis racket into the snowbank 10 feet away from the basketball net. A very brave leprechaun then put on a helmet and climbed onto the racket. Lying down on his back he stretched his arms out to the side and grasped the racket with his hands. The count down began. Ten, nine, eight, seven, six, five, four

(I pulled the racket back, back, back) three, two, one, blast off! I let go of the racket, the leprechaun went flying up and up and up and... if he steered himself correctly in the air, he went swish, right through the basketball net! RIGHT THROUGH THE NET! Then I had to run and catch him before he hit the ground. Whew - it was amazing!

Throughout the events, some of the crowds of spectators lined the branches of the trees, high off the ground. What a view they had! And could they make noise! It was all so much fun. Yes, it was a wonderful adventure, this "new" old house.

BEST FRIENDS

Our time together at the "new" old house lasted for many years. Winters were filled with campfires and races, tapping trees for sap, and of course, St. Patrick's Days. Rosie delivered all kinds of news; the rolled up paper tied carefully around her neck was such a fun way to hear of new babies, new houses, new roofs and new friends. Springs and summers were my favorite times with the leprechauns though; their mischief and magic seemed to keep the woods alive with surprises. And Mr. McAllister was the best friend a person could hope for. He was funny and kind, and if he ever did get mad, he'd stamp his feet so hard and so fast, that it was almost funny. His little cheeks would get very red, his white hair would flop all over, and the buckles on his boots would sparkle in the sun as he stamped, and shook his fists during his little temper tantrums. There was never anything horrible to make him mad, just the things that made him frustrated... like ladders that tipped over with him on them, or campfires that wouldn't stay lit, or little kids who insisted on playing tricks of their own on him.

Our yard was a peaceful place and our "new" old house became a home; everything was just as we had hoped it would be. The neighbors never knew about the leprechauns that lived in our woods. It was a secret we promised to keep and we did. But there was always some sort of trickery going on, and no one could ever figure it out. Flowers would pop out of the winter snow and our neighbor thought she was seeing things. The fish in the creek would jump up out of the water, flap their fins and spit water at the fishermen on shore, just to tease them. The fishermen would look, then look again, rub their eyes but when they looked back everything was back to normal. Mr. McAllister would always tell me about his tricks and would hold his round belly and laugh till he cried.

SO LONG FOR A WHILE

We've lived in this house for almost eleven years now. It's decision time again, but this time the decision was made for us, we had no choice. My husband's job is moving to a new city. Our kids are all grown up and are away at college, so it makes this move a little easier. Moving to the city means - no old farmhouse, no big backyard, and no woods.

This time the leprechauns will stay and we will leave. When I told Mr. McAllister the news he was sad, but he knows that I am a true friend, a forever friend. I'll still come to visit, I'll still laugh at his tricks, I'll still feel wonderful when I smell the pussy willow torches and the bubbling stew. And when I visit at night, I'll smile as I walk the path with fireflies lighting the way. We both know that they are safe for ever and ever in our woods. Safe from bulldozers and trucks, these woods - forever tall, and green, and theirs.

So today is moving day, again. The boxes and furniture are in the truck. The neighbors are all here to say good-bye. As I hug each of them, I look over their shoulders to see if Mr. McAllister is coming down the path from the backyard. I have to see him before I leave... just one more time. Another hug, another peek... and there he is, walking slowly. I can feel the tears starting to fill my eyes.

My neighbors each walk away and wave their final good-byes. I know we'll see them soon. I also know they don't see Mr. McAllister, no more than ten inches tall, my little forever friend.

He stops at the beginning of the path as if an invisible wall keeps him from stepping onto the grass of the backyard. He motions for me to come over and looks as sad as I feel, but we both know that this time is different. It's all ok, and just a little sad to say good bye.

"Big One," he says, "this home is better than we dreamed it could be. We're happy here and safe. And it's all thanks to you. How can we ever thank you for this?"

"Mr. McAllister, you don't have to thank me. There was never a question that we'd stay together. You've made our lives happy, too. So, thank YOU," I said. "And now it's time for us to go. I won't say good bye... just so long for a while."

"Then, so long for a while, Big One - but please promise it will be a short while. Come back to visit soon."

"I will, I promise."

"Pinky swear?"

"Pinky swear," I said as I held up my pinky and knelt on the ground next to him. He wrapped his tiny pinky around mine and sealed it with a kiss.

"Then be gone with ya... and beware of leprechaun magic. We're everywhere, ya know."

"I know," I laughed, "believe me I know."

He headed down the path, only turning once to look back and wave. I blew him a kiss that landed on a light breeze and floated softly to him.

He caught it, smiled, stuffed it in his pocket and in a poof ... he disappeared.

THE END

ACKNOWLEDGEMENTS

My deepest thanks to Tess Holloway for her time, her thoughts and her amazing insights. I knew I could count on her to do a thorough review, and I wasn't disappointed. She was a talented "field consultant", whose detailed notes I'll keep for years to come. When she's famous, I can pull them out and say, "I knew her when..."

With happy memories flying around, I must thank Mak and Jess for their help filming the Leprechaun Olympics. I couldn't have recorded that wonderful day without them!

To Mr. McAllister for trusting me with his friendship. It's been so much fun getting to know a silly, little leprechaun!

Sandy Barton is a retired elementary school teacher from Buffalo, New York. She loved telling her students at Forest Elementary about the leprechauns in her back woods, and watching them come back year after year on St. Patrick's Day to catch a glimpse of that tricky little man.

Sandy is the author of *Abjectedly Yours*, an adult memoir. It is co-authored with Anthony Chandor, another dear, very unlikely friend from Bath, UK.

Visit SandyBarton.com for more information, or to contact her about author visits. Thanks for reading Discovery in the Woods. Keep believing in the magic!

CPSIA information can be obtained at www.ICGtesting.com
Printed in the USA
LVOW11s1142090314

376608LV00006B/739/P